Bink and Slinky's
Ark Adventure

Written by
Donna Arlynn Frisinger

Illustrated by
Monica Gutierrez

Blessings on Your
Journey. Love,
Donna Frisinger

(Prov. 3:5&6)
"Trust in the Lord..."

2013

Standard
PUBLISHING
Cincinnati, Ohio

Published by Standard Publishing, Cincinnati, Ohio
www.standardpub.com

Text Copyright © 2013 by Donna Arlynn Frisinger
Illustrations Copyright © 2013 by Standard Publishing

Printed in: China
Artist: Monica Gutierrez
Cover and interior design: Sandy Wimmer and Andrew Quach

ISBN 978-0-7847-3688-3

Library of Congress Cataloging-in-Publication Data
Frisinger, Donna Arlynn.
 Bink and Slinky's ark adventure / written by Donna Arlynn Frisinger ; illustrated by Monica Gutierrez.
   p. cm.
 Summary: When two small snails are called by God to find and board an ark, they trust God will provide a way and, through the help of many animals, they reach their destination in time.
 ISBN 978-0-7847-3688-3
[1. Stories in rhyme. 2. Voyages and travels--Fiction. 3. Snails--Fiction. 4. Animals--Fiction. 5. Faith--Fiction. 6. Noah's ark--Fiction.] I. Gutierrez, Monica (Monica Graciela), 1960- ill. II. Title.
 PZ8.3.F91787Bin 2013
 [E]--dc23
         2012030965

18 17 16 15 14 13   1 2 3 4 5 6 7 8 9

Faith means . . . knowing that something is real
even if we do not see it (Hebrews 11:1).

For my Barry—
Whose persistence captured my heart . . .
Till death do us part.
Thanks for taking the journey with me.
                              —Donna

What is this strange message two groovy snails found
at the Garden of Chewies, in slime on the ground?

Dear Bink and Slinky,
Get out of this garden. Leave before dark.
The Great Falling is coming. Go find Noah's ark.
Your shack's on your back. You will need nothing more.
Slime up your sneakers—your feet may get sore.
—God
PS. Get going.

So Bink and Slinky each stuck a foot out
to begin their journey without fear or doubt.

"So long, everybody!
Arrivederci! Au revoir!

Toodle-oo! See ya later!
Farewell! Ta-ta!

Hasta la vista! Sayonara! Adieu! Good-bye!
Adios! Aloha! Bon voyage! Don't cry."

Garden
of Chewies

Meanwhile their parents packed them a lunch
of leaf stems and flowers to snicky-snack crunch.

"But where is this ark?" said Bink's Mom and Pop.
"Do you have a map? Do you know where to stop?"

"Not yet," Bink answered. "But when God calls, you *go*."
They all gave a hug and waved. "Cheerio!"

They squirmed and they wormed. Then Bink yelled, "A river!"
They looked at each other . . . A quiver. A shiver.

"Oh no!" said Slinky. "What will we do?"
"Don't know," said Bink. "We need a canoe."

Suddenly a splashing of gurgles and swirls
and two blinking eyeballs like emerald-green pearls.

"Yoo-hoo! Mister Crocodile, over here, sir!
The water is deep. We need a chauffeur!

We must get to the ark. May we hitch a ride?"
Sir Crocodile smiled. "Inch aboard my backside."

Then Bink and Slinky slid over his scales,
singing the fearless song of two snails.

"We slide, we glide,

we're grooving side by side.

We don't know where we're going,

but we know God will provide."

Aaaaah-choo!

In time they slimed to a dry desert place.
The blistering sand stopped their one-footed race.

"Oh no!" said Slinky. "We'll sizzle and bake!
My house is too heavy. I have a backache."
"Don't worry," said Bink. "We'll rest at daybreak."

Just then . . . in moonlight . . . a snort and a wheeze.
A humpy-backed animal spluttered and sneezed.

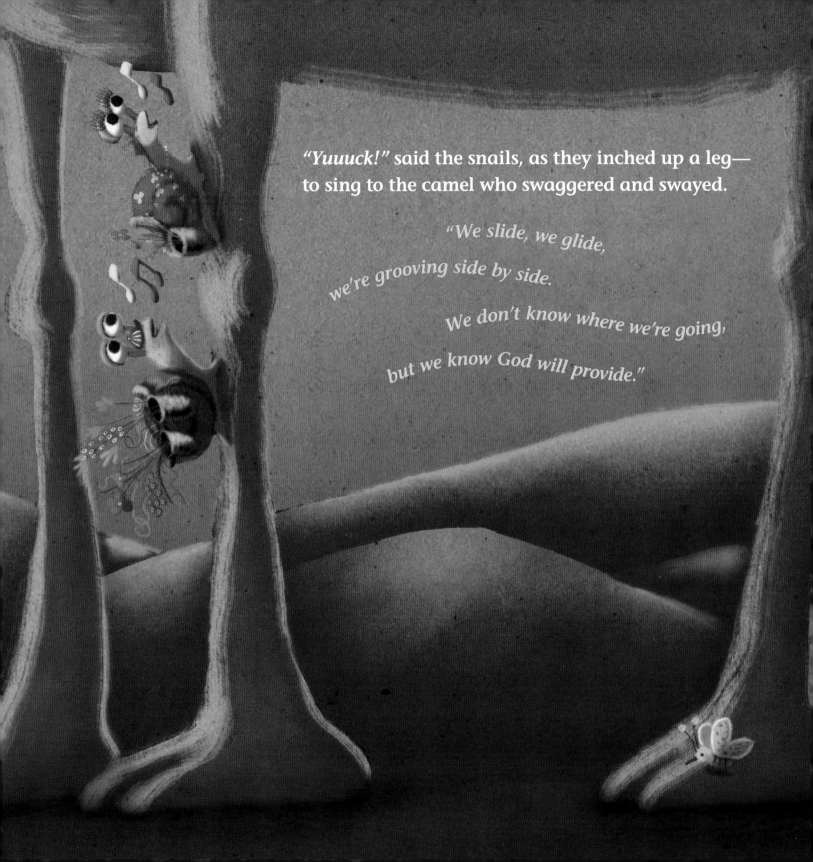

"Yuuuck!" said the snails, as they inched up a leg—
to sing to the camel who swaggered and swayed.

"We slide, we glide,

we're grooving side by side.

We don't know where we're going,

but we know God will provide."

Uh-oh! A jungle . . . the beat of a drum!
A swallowing swamp filled with slithering scum.

"Oh my!" cried Slinky. "What will we do?"
"Don't know," answered Bink. "I'll leave that to you."

They swished through the trees
on a flying trapeze,
squealing and praying,
"Please, God, help us pleeease!"

After many more days, they came to a mountain—
a rumble like thunder, the gush of a fountain.

In the darkness of shadows came a flapping of wings,
soaring and swooping to eat snaily things!

"Yikes!" screamed Slinky. "Scrunch into your shell!"
Hearts beating, they peeked out to see . . .

. . . all was well.

"You can nestle in my wings," a bald eagle said.
"My quilt is quite soft. You'll like your new bed."

And Bink and Slinky did!

By now, alas, a whole year had passed.
No sign of an ark—not even the mast.

"Maybe there is no such thing. We could die!"
"Don't know," panted Bink. "But we've got to try."

"But no one has heard of a thing called Great Falling.
How do we know this is really *God* calling?

Can't see it. Can't touch it. Can't smell it at all!
How do we know what we know? We're *sooo* small."

Then just in the nick of two tiny snails' time—
just when they started to run out of slime . . .

Who came a-loping,
but Madame Giraffe.
They inched up her neck.
They squiggled and laughed!

For there up ahead—
glory be!—in the grass
was a big wooden boat.
They'd found it at last!

At that moment a plopping drop-dripped to the ground.
Plunk-plunk . . . plunk-plunk . . . It plopped all around.

Amid stomping, stampeding, grunt-groaning, it fell.
A man they called Noah jumped up with a yell.

"Pull up the plank. The Great Falling's begun!
Get moving! Get cracking. Now shake a leg. *Run!*"

Bink and Slinky double-timed their song.

"We slide, we glide,
we're grooving side by side.
We don't know where we're going,
but we know God will provide."

The snails finally made it aboard Noah's ark.
They sailed monster waves in the crackling dark.

It rained, and it stormed. It *howled,* and it *roared*!
The waters rose higher, and still the rain poured.

When forty days ended, the Great Falling stopped.
Still more snail-days later, the plank creaked and dropped.

And when all God's creatures left the ark that day . . .

And sang all the way!

"We slide, we glide,
we're grooving side by side.
We don't know where we're going,
but we know God will provide."

But now . . .

What is *this* message that's dazzling the sky,
sparkling in clouds, with a rainbow up high?

Dear Bink and Slinky,

Bravo! Well done!

Nice going! What fun!

Through high places, dry places, creeping strange trails,

your faith in my Word saved the future of snails.

—God